THIS IS HULK

Adapted by Chris "Doc" Wyatt

Illustrated by Ron Lim and Rachelle Rosenberg

Based on the Marvel comic book series The Avengers

Los Angeles
New York

© 2015 MARVEL

Printed in China
First Box Set Edition, April 2015
7 9 10 8 6
FAC-025393-19245
ISBN 978-1-4847-2179-7
Not for individual resale

This is Hulk.

The Hulk is the strongest!
The Hulk is the biggest!

Hulk gets mad when bad guys try
to hurt good people.
He protects good people.

The madder the Hulk gets,
the stronger he gets.

The Hulk likes to say
"HULK SMASH"!
He is very good
at smashing things.

Hulk looks different
from other heroes.
Some people think
he is a monster.

The Hulk is sad when people treat
him like a monster.

Yet the Hulk still protects people.

He even helps the ones
who are mean to him.

The Hulk is not always strong.

Sometimes he is Bruce Banner.
Bruce Banner is a scientist.

One day, before he was the Hulk,
Bruce was testing a bomb.

Oh, no!
Someone walked into the test!

Bruce had to help.

He jumped in.
He saved the boy.
But he got blasted!

The blast turned Bruce
into the Hulk!

At first Bruce was scared.
He looked like a monster.

He found out the Hulk
can be good, too.
The Hulk can be a hero!

Whenever Bruce gets very mad,
he grows big and strong.

He turns into the Hulk!

Evildoers should fear the Hulk.

Good people do not have to worry.

An army general
wants to stop the Hulk.

But he will not.

Now the Hulk helps the Avengers.

The Hulk lives in Avengers Tower.

The Hulk and Thor
are best friends.

With the Avengers or alone,
the Hulk is always a Super Hero!